ORLAND PARK PUBLIC LIBRARY
3 1315 00531 1902

P9-EMG-475

In loving memory of my gentle mother, Anne.
And for my big brother, James.

Library of Congress Cataloging-in-Publication Data available.
ISBN 978-0-8118-6908-9

Book design by Amy E. Achaibou.
Typeset in Rockwell.
The illustrations in this book were rendered in gouache.

Manufactured by Toppan Leefung, Da Ling Shan Town,
Dongguan, China, in December 2009.

10 9 8 7 6 5 4 3 2 1

This product conforms to CPSIA 2008.

Chronicle Books LLC
680 Second Street, San Francisco, California 94107

www.chroniclekids.com

One Too Many

A Seek & Find Counting Book

Gianna Marino

chronicle books · san francisco

1

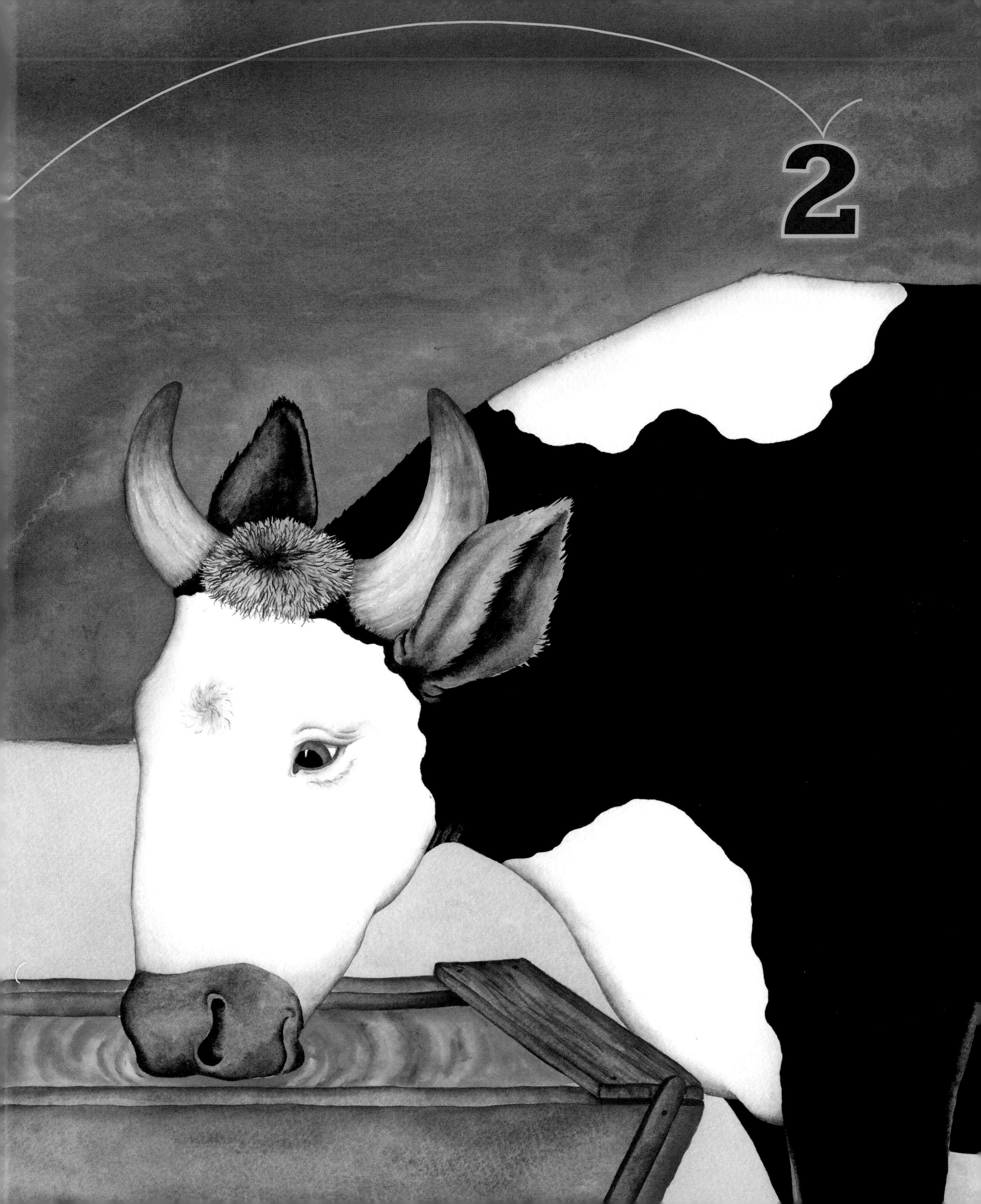
2

3

4

5

6

7

8

9

10

11

12

plus one more
equals . . .

one too many!

1 Flea
2 Cows
3 Horses
4 Goats
5 Sheep
6 Pigs
7 Bunnies
8 Geese
9 Chickens
10 Mice
11 Fireflies
12 Bats
1 Skunk
Total number of animals from pages 1 through 12: 364; plus one more equals 365!

To keep the fun going, try these extra seek-and-find challenges!

- Search for the pig that always gets his ear nibbled on.
- Find the rabbit that likes to climb on the other animals.
- Count all the animals on each page.
- Search for the animals that have their eyes closed.
- Find the goose that pops up from the bottom to look at you.
- Count the total number of animals from pages 1 through 12.

What else can you search, find, or count?

ANSWERS: Number of animals on each page from 1 through 12: 1, 3, 6, 10, 15, 21, 28, 36, 45, 55, 66, 78; plus one more equals 79!